Ben's Birthdays

Elizabeth Hawkins
Illustrated by Paul Cemmick

Tamarind

BEN'S BIRTHDAYS
TAMARIND BOOKS 978 1 848 53018 8

Published in Great Britain by Tamarind Books,
a division of Random House Children's Books
A Random House Group Company

This edition published 2010

1 3 5 7 9 10 8 6 4 2

Text copyright © Elizabeth Hawkins, 2010
Illustrations copyright © Paul Cemmick, 2010

TAMARIND BOOKS
61–63 Uxbridge Road, London, W5 5SA

www.**tamarindbooks**.co.uk
www.**kids**at**randomhouse**.co.uk
www.**rbooks**.co.uk

Addresses for companies within The Random House Group Limited
can be found at: www.**randomhouse**.co.uk/offices.htm
THE RANDOM HOUSE GROUP Limited Reg. No. 954009

A CIP catalogue record for this book is available from
the British Library.
Printed in China

To Debbie and Jeremy
E.H.

To Mum, Dave, Sarah, Lucas,
Marina, Rosie and Woody
P.C.

Chapter One
WHEN'S MY BIRTHDAY?

"Is it my birthday?" asked Ben each day, as he sat down to breakfast.

"No, silly!" laughed his sister Jessica.

"It's never my birthday," Ben sighed and munched his cereal.

"Birthdays come only once a year," said Mum. "Your birthday was in the summer."

"No!" groaned Ben. "I can't wait that long."

"Jessica's birthday will be next," Mum went on.

A few weeks later, Mum took Ben shopping to buy a present for his sister Jessica.

Ben felt glum. "How long until *my* birthday, Mum?" he asked.

"Quite a long time, dear. Your birthday is in the summer, remember?"

The next morning Ben went downstairs for breakfast. Mum and Dad were busy getting everything ready for Jessica's birthday. There was a huge pile of presents and cards on the table, and they were all for Jessica.

When Jessica bounced into the kitchen, everything was ready.

"Happy birthday, Jessica!" said Mum and Dad.

"What about me? Is there anything for me?" asked Ben.

"Of course not, Ben!" said Jessica. "It's not *your* birthday."

Ben gave Jessica the box of fudge he had bought with his mother. "Happy birthday, Jessica," he said sadly. "But when is *my* birthday?"

"Don't be silly, Ben," said Dad. "It's not so long since your last birthday."

Chapter Two
IT'S NOT FAIR!

"How many birthdays have you had?" Ben asked
Dad one day.

"Let me think… I have had thirty-eight birthdays."

"And how many birthdays has Mum had?"
asked Ben.

"Thirty-six," said Dad.

"And Jessica has had ten birthdays," moaned Ben.
"But I have only had six. Everyone has had more
than me. It's not fair!"

"But Ben, you can't hurry birthdays," explained Dad. "They come when it's the right time."

Ben pulled a face and groaned.

"Listen. I can explain how long it will be until your birthday," said Dad. "It's autumn now and the leaves are turning gold and falling. Winter will follow, with dark evenings and frost and snow. After that comes spring, with pale new leaves and pink blossom on the cherry trees. Then the sun will warm up so that the grass and flowers grow. That will be summer and you will have your birthday."

But Ben was not happy. "I can't wait that long," he said.

Chapter Three
DON'T SQUASH ME!

Ben went off to school feeling sad and cross. Jessica danced along in the shiny new shoes Grandma had sent for her birthday. On her back was her smart new school bag from Mum and Dad.

Ben dragged his feet and stared at the pavement.

"Pick your feet up!" squeaked a little voice down by his boots. "Don't squash me!"

Ben bent down. A snail was crawling across the pavement.

"Help me across before someone squashes me," said the squeaky voice.

"A talking snail?" said Ben amazed as he peered at the curly, round shell.

"Pick me up. Put me somewhere safe where I will not get squashed."

"Come along, Ben," called Mum. "You are getting left behind."

So Ben, being a kind boy, picked up the snail and popped it in his pocket.

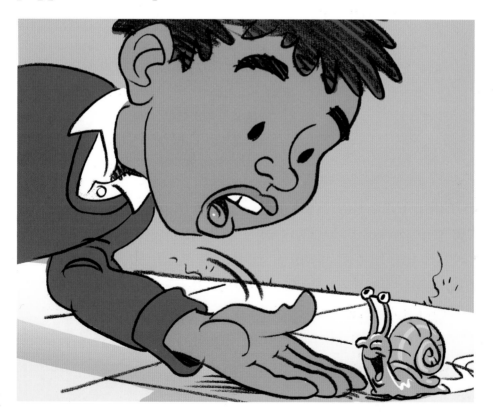

Chapter Four
BEN'S WISH

All day long Ben took care of the snail. At playtime the snail asked Ben to put him somewhere damp.

"It's too hot in your pocket," it moaned. "Snails like being cool and wet."

So Ben found a dripping drain pipe in the playground and the snail took a cool shower.

At lunchtime the snail was hungry, so Ben shared a piece of his apple.

When Ben arrived home that evening he took
the snail out of his pocket.

"Whatever is that snail doing on the kitchen table?"
said Mum. "Take it out to the garden, Ben."

"Quite right too," squeaked the snail. "I would like
a shady crack in your garden wall."

It was not difficult finding a big enough crack in the
old brick wall.

"This will do very nicely, thank you," said the snail,
snuggling deep into the crack. "It's sheltered from
the wind and frost, so if you don't mind… I will go
to sleep now."

"Do you want me to wake you up in the morning?"
asked Ben.

"Heavens no!" said the snail. "I shall sleep until
the spring when the juicy new leaves appear."

"But that's ages," said Ben. "Dad said winter
comes first with dark evenings and frost and snow."

"Exactly," said the snail. "Snails don't like
the winter, so they go to sleep. Now, you have been
such a kind, helpful child, I think I will allow you
one small wish."

"A wish! Anything I want?" said Ben, astonished.

"Anything you want. But choose quickly," yawned
the snail. "I'm very sleepy."

Ben didn't need to think about it. "I want my birthday," he said.

"When do you want your birthday?" said the sleepy snail.

"When?" thought Ben, puzzled. He could not think which day.

The snail's head was drooping.

"Every day!" shouted Ben.

The snail nodded, drew tight into its shell and fell fast asleep.

Chapter Five
A BIRTHDAY

"Happy Birthday, Ben!" said Mum the next day
when he came down to breakfast.

On the table was a pile of presents. From Mum
there was a football shirt, from Dad a model
spaceship kit, and from Jessica a yellow, bouncy ball.

Then the postman called and from Grandma
there was a stripy, woolly scarf.

"Wow!" said Ben. "It's my birthday!"

He wore his football shirt to school under his
jumper. He wrapped his stripy scarf round his neck
and tucked his yellow ball under his arm. He had fun
kicking the ball with his friends in the playground.

After school his friends crowded round.

"We are coming to your party," they said.

Mum took them all to the park. They had a football
game and a picnic tea of crisps, little sausages,
chocolate biscuits and Ben's favourite lemon cake,
with Mum's icing on top.

"That was a lovely party, Mum," said Ben
that night.

13

Ben started making his spaceship but very soon it was bed time.

"You can finish it tomorrow," said Mum, as she tucked Ben into bed.

Chapter Six
NOT ANOTHER!

Ben woke up with the rain pattering on his bedroom window. He dressed and went down to breakfast.

"Happy birthday, Ben!" sighed Mum.

On the table was another heap of presents. From Mum there were football boots, from Dad a kit for a model plane and from Jessica a red, bouncy ball.

Then the postman called and from Grandma there was a stripy, woolly hat.

"What a lot of presents!" said Ben.

On the way to school he wore his stripy scarf and hat but the rain made them soggy. He tucked his yellow ball under one arm and his red ball under the other.

Mrs Chang said, "One ball is quite enough for playtime, Ben. Leave the red ball in the tray on my desk."

After school Ben's friends crowded round.

"Why are you having another party?" they said.

As it was raining Dad took them all to the cinema.
They had ice creams and popcorn and chocolate bars
and fizzy drinks.

Then they went home to Ben's house to have
a slice of Ben's favourite lemon birthday cake,
with Mum's icing on top.

That night Ben decided to finish his spaceship later. Instead he built half his model aeroplane.

Then Mum said, "Time for bed, Ben. Put away your aeroplane kit. You can finish it tomorrow."

That night Ben had a tummy ache, but Mum was too busy making a cake in the kitchen to hear when he called.

Chapter Seven
DO WE HAVE TO COME?

"Happy birthday, Ben!" yawned Mum the next day when Ben came down to breakfast.

On the table was another heap of presents. From Mum there was a football track suit, from Dad there was a train set, and from Jessica there was a blue, bouncy ball.

When the postman called there was an enormous pair of stripy, woolly gloves from Gran.

"More presents," said Ben quietly.

It was difficult walking to school clutching three balls and wearing huge, floppy gloves.

"Three balls today. That's far too many!" said Mrs Chang. "Give them all to me. I will lock them in the cupboard until going home time."

After school Ben's friends crowded round.

"Do we have to come to your swimming party?" they said.

"I'm going to miss my favourite TV programme," said Amy.

"I have not played on my computer all week," complained Tom.

"Why do you always have parties?" asked Chantelle.

Ben was a good swimmer, but today he didn't feel like swimming. He wanted to go home on his own and finish building his spaceship, paint his aeroplane and lay out his train set.

Afterwards the children had a birthday tea at Ben's house. They ate crisps and peanuts, jam Swiss rolls and doughnuts. They drank sticky, fizzy, cherry drink and they finished Ben's favourite lemon birthday cake, with Mum's icing on top.

But Ben didn't want any lemon birthday cake. He felt sick at the sight of birthday food. He longed for an ordinary supper of rice and peas, or fried eggs and bacon, or pasta and tomato sauce.

Chapter Eight
I HATE BIRTHDAYS

The birthdays didn't stop! Mum and Dad forgot to tuck Ben up at night. They were busy cooking birthday food or late-night shopping for presents.

Dad put up rows and rows of hooks for his new football kits.

Ben's drawers were bursting with woolly hats, scarves, gloves and even thick socks, knitted by Grandma. His mattress was lumpy because there were so many balls squashed underneath the bed.

Ben never had any time to finish his spaceship, or paint his model aeroplane, or lay out his train set. They got buried under a set of prancing knights on horses, an airport, a fire engine that had lost its firemen, the pieces of a jigsaw…

"I'm fed up with birthdays," Ben decided. "I don't enjoy them any more. I will find that snail and ask it to take my wish back."

Out in the garden, Ben pushed his fingers into the crack in the wall. He could not find the snail anywhere.

So the birthdays went on… and on… and on… and Ben hated them more and more.

The house was always a mess because everyone was too tired to tidy up before the next party. There was never any breakfast. Mum and Dad had to buy so much party food that there was no money left for breakfast cereal or orange juice.

As for Ben, he had no time to enjoy his presents and play quietly in his room. He could not walk across his bedroom floor without stumbling and crunching on presents. They covered the floor, the shelves, the window sill… They were spreading all over his bed.

He had so much of everything that he didn't notice any of it.

Chapter Nine
TOO MUCH OF A GOOD THING

Then one winter's day, Ben spotted the snail's eyes poking out of a crack in the garden wall.

"Help!" Ben shouted into the crack. "Wake up! It's me, Ben. You gave me the wish and…"

"There's no need to shout," came a sleepy, squeaky voice. "I'm peeping out for a little fresh air before I go back to sleep. It's not spring yet. I will talk to you then."

"Don't go back to sleep!" cried Ben. "Please don't sleep until you have stopped my birthdays."

"So it's the birthdays, is it?" squeaked the snail. "Too much of a good thing, eh?"

"Just one birthday a year is plenty, thank you," said Ben quickly.

"I understand," said the snail, looking more awake. "When I sleep I dream of the juicy new leaves I will eat in spring. If I had green leaves to eat all winter, the spring leaves would not be special."

The next morning Ben came downstairs to breakfast and there were no presents.

"Hurry up, Ben, it's nearly time for school," said Mum.

"See you tonight," called Dad as he left for work.

"Is my lunch box ready, Mum?" asked Jessica.

That day the postman didn't call at all.

When Ben came home from school that night all the presents had disappeared from his room. He didn't mind.

He got out his felt tips and drew a picture of a bulldozer, while Mum cooked egg and sausage for his tea.

After tea, Ben watched TV with Jessica. Then Dad read him a story and Mum tucked him up in bed.

That night, in his tidy room, Ben lay in bed thinking. For his next birthday would he like a space station, or maybe a pirate ship with model pirates? Or would a bicycle be more fun? He could not decide.

Luckily, there was still plenty of time to dream and plan.

Ben decided that waiting for his next birthday was going to be fun after all.

TAMARIND READERS

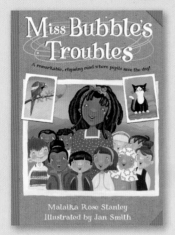

Miss Bubble's Troubles
by *Malaika Rose Stanley*
Illustrated by Jan Smith

Miss Bubble is a super-cool teacher at Topley Primary School. The children in Rainbow Class have lots of fun with her. When Miss Bubble ends up in a spot of trouble, her parrot Shriek and cat Milkshake try their best to help. But they need Rainbow Class to come to the rescue...
A rhyming story about a great teacher and her class.

Spike and Ali Enson
by *Malaika Rose Stanley*
Illustrated by Sarah Horne

Everyone loves Spike's baby brother, Ali. But Spike thinks there's definitely something strange about him. Ali's poos are bright green and his soft, brown skin looks scaly.
When Spike discovers a way to learn the truth about Ali, he begins to realise just how different his family really is...
A hilarious story for children who can read fluently on their own.

Reading Between the Lions
by *Gillian Swordy*
Illustrated by Leighton Noyes

Lionel is being bullied at school but he gets some great advice from two friendly stone lions in his garden.
This rhyming romp is perfect for young readers just starting to read on their own.

Ferris Fleet: the Wheelchair Wizard
by Annie Dalton
Illustrated by Carl Pearce
When Oscar's mum has to go away for work she looks for a baby-sitter and finds Ferris Fleet, a wizard in a wheelchair.
A futuristic space story for readers who are comfortable reading on their own.

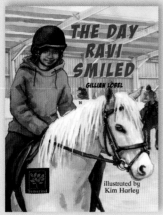

The Day Ravi Smiled
by Gillian Lobel
Illustrated by Kim Harley
Joy rides at Penniwells Riding Centre. There is a boy there called Ravi who doesn't talk. Joy worries about him. She doesn't know he's autistic. One day Joy needs Ravi's help...
A great story about a riding school for children with disabilities. For children who are starting to read on their own.

Hurricane
by Verna Wilkins
Illustrated by Tim Clarey
Live through a hurricane on a Caribbean island with Troy and Nita.
An exciting adventure story for children who can read fluently on their own.

To find out about the rest of our list, go to
www.tamarindbooks.co.uk